Annie Cabannie's
Star Baby

Written by
Sylvestra Throckmorton

Illustrated by
Benjamin Fritsch
Sylvestra Throckmorton

Annie Cabannie's Star Baby
By Sylvestra Throckmorton - 1st Ed.

Illustration by Benjamin Fritsch and
Sylvestra Throckmorton

ISBN 0-9761723-0-5

Printed in Korea

Publisher
A.S. Greene & Company
1828 Kings Highway
Lincoln Park, MI 48146

To my precious daughters,
Marissa-Tate and Mayci-Rose,

This is the story of how we came to be
together as a family.

All my love,
Momma

A special thanks to the friends and family
that support and love us.

A very heartfelt thanks to Bernice and Eston Goodell
for stepping in as the Grandparents that my children
would have never had.

Eternal gratitude to Grandma Madeleine Goldstein
for also stepping in as "Grandma"
but mostly thank you for all that you do for us.
We love you!

Thank you, Grammy Angel and Papa Boy for making
All of this possible.

There once was a lady named Annie Cabannie
She had lots of cats but not enough family
Of children she had none, not a single one.
"I need something more
Than to mother these cats.
If I don't have a family, I'm sure to go bats!"

Friends said, "You're crazy,
You've already gone bats.
You're so old, it's too hard,
You've got all those cats!"

It's true that her life
Was just fine as it was,
Annie yearned for much more
Than some purring and paws.

She ached for a family to call her own
So come what may, near or far she would roam.
Very certain that this was her destiny,
"Somewhere there's a baby
That needs a Mommy like me!"

She thought, "To a baby I will find my way,
Though I don't know how I'll do that today"
Every night to the stars she would gaze.
Up she'd look and she would say,

"Star Baby, no matter where you are,
No matter where you land,
I will find you, kiss you, and hold your sweet hand.
I hope you hear this little plea
To just hold on
'Til we can be
Together as a family."

Annie's mom, an angel on high,
Said down to Annie from up in the sky,
"I will lead you to your little girl,
Even if it's way 'round the world.
So just hold on and you will see,
You will have your family."

Annie went to Morning Star,
For they found babies near and far.
"Please write here and over there,
Up and down and everywhere.
Now fill this out and have no doubt,
Babies are what we're all about."

Time after time skyward Annie would say,
"Please Momma Angel, point the way
To the star that will fall as my baby someday."
Every night to the stars in the sky,
Annie would whisper her lullaby.

"Star Baby, no matter where you are,
No matter where you land,
I will find you, kiss you, and hold your sweet hand.
I hope you hear this little plea
To just hold on
'Til we can be
Together as a family."

Time dragged on and Annie felt sad,
Even though things weren't really so bad.
She phoned the folks at the agency
Who said, "We've got pictures and you might see
A baby for your family."

Annie declared, "I'm stuck at work
And can't leave 'til four.
Could you please leave the pictures
Taped to your door?"

The day seemed endless, she needed to race,
To see those pictures,
Would she know the right face?

One magical smile and that's all it took.
She picked out her baby with one little look!

Nightly, Annie would look up to the Moon
That would smile
Over her, over all, and her Star Baby child.
"Now that I've seen my sweet little girl,
Please shine down this message
Even 'way round the world."

"Star Baby, the same moon and stars
Shine down on us both.
They carry my message,
My sincere heartfelt oath
To find you and love you
I promise we'll be
Together real soon
As a new family."

And now that she knew who her baby would be,
Annie would travel over land and sea
To the place where her Star Baby fell to earth
Antigua, Guatemala, the place of her birth.

Auntie Jannie took Annie Cabannie
To the airport to fly away
To bring back Star Baby to her new home in Redford,
Where she'd happily grow, learn, and play.
Annie sat on the plane, scared out of her wits,
She wondered and hoped it would be a good fit.
"There's no turning back now. I must be brave.
Let me be a good Mommy," to God she would pray.

Dressed in white, a most beautiful sight,
Star Baby could finally go home!
Together they'd fly
Cross the world through the sky
And never again be alone.

Annie Cabannie named her new daughter, Frannie,
Then left to go home on their flight.
Although her arms never left her sweet baby,
Annie still ached to hold Frannie tight.

Family and friends waited to greet her,
All were excited to hug her and meet her.
A party with presents, balloons, cake, and signs
Planned for Annie and Frannie,
A total surprise!

They lived happily ever after, well almost you see...
They loved each other but wanted more family.
Now Annie Cabannie and her little girl, Frannie,
Nightly lifted their eyes to the sky.
"Dear Grammy Angel, your first match was perfect,
So there's something we'd like you to try.
We need a sister to add to our midst.
We'll love her, and feed her,
And make sure she's kissed."
When they were certain
That Grammy had heard,
Together they sang out these comforting words.

"Star Baby, no matter where you are,
No matter where you land,
We'll find you, kiss you, and hold your sweet hand.
We hope you hear this little plea
To just hold on
'Til we can be
Together as a family of three!"

Friends said, "You're crazy,
You've gone totally bats.
You're so old, it's too hard.
You've a daughter and cats!"

It's true that her life
Was just fine as it was.
Frannie yearned for much more
Than some purring and paws.

She ached for a sister to call her own.
So come what may, near and far they would roam.
Very certain that this was their destiny,
"Somewhere there's a baby
That needs Mommy and Me!"

One year later....

Thanks, Grammy Angel, Great Job, AGAIN!"

To those people "on the fence" about adoption. My words of encouragement and advice.

Dear Fencers,

Follow your heart, which might not initially coincide with reason. This will be your most exhilarating and thrilling adventure but one of the most difficult and challenging things you will ever do. Your strength and sanity will be tested repeatedly both before and after the adoption. However, your strength will grow ten fold and your sanity will be cultivated to a new level of clarity. Without children, life is just existence and survival... Bring children into your life and now you are really LIVING!

The waiting is agonizing and each day seems like one hundred but when you finally hold that baby in your arms, the agony blossoms into joy that is beyond description.

Go for it!

Educate yourself. Do your homework and talk to every knowledgeable person possible. Investigate and verify the legitimacy of all sources. After you've done all that please consider the magnitude of this lifetime commitment. If your heart and intellect still ache for a baby, get your support systems in place and...

Go for it!

You've probably guessed by now that I am the real-life Annie Cabannie and every word of this story is true. My miracle babies have made me grow as a human being and constantly make me strive to be a better and braver person.

God Bless you and I wish you the very best with your "new" family.

To those people "on the fence"
About being adopted.
My words of encouragement and advice.

Dear Fencers,

Please be reassured that you are incredibly special human beings and that your parents went to the ends of the earth to make you a part of their family. You were wanted more than words could say and loved before they even met you, just like biological children. However, with biological children, sometimes parents do not make the choice to increase their family numbers. You were a very deliberate choice, a very well planned choice. Your parents went to phenomenal lengths to follow through on that decision. Nothing about the process was frivolous or easy.

Remember, everything in life happens the way it is supposed to. You were meant for the family you were adopted by. I tell my children that they were stars in the sky and then fell to earth as babies. They landed in another lady's tummy because mine couldn't hold a baby. Then I went to get them because they were supposed to be with me! I call them my "miracle babies." I wasn't able to have children for many different reasons and NOW I HAVE CHILDREN!!! How much more incredible can that be?

You are loved, wanted, and appreciated more than any words can describe. Everything you do is monumental. All that I do has greater meaning and purpose because now I do it for a family. Do what you need to do to make peace with yourself and your family. What a miracle it is that from all over the world, people bond together so lovingly. Take into account how very blessed you are!

Enjoy your blessings!